MONSTERS ON THE LOOSE

Michael Chesworth

Troll

To anyone who remembers
Kishacoquillas Park

In a small amusement park on Lake Wumpapomac, an odd thing happened. It all began when Dr. Fear, owner of Dr. Fear's Fun House of Astounding Horror, decided to take a vacation.

"Pago Pago, here I come," Dr. Fear sang. "Two weeks of fun in the sun!"

The creatures watched Dr. Fear as he walked out the front door, locking it behind him.

"How do you like that?" said Boris, the vampire. "He gets a vacation, and we have to stay in this boring old fun house!"

Vulture agreed. "It's really rather unfair!"

"Yeah," said Frankie sadly. "No fair!"

"Well, I won't take this," said Spike, the skeleton, angrily. "What do you say we bust out of here, guys?"

"Yahoo!" they all cheered together.

"I'll pick the lock with my pinkie finger bone," said Spike.

But Fang, the T-rex, couldn't wait. He made a door of his own right through the wall.

The creatures squinted their eyes in the bright sunlight as they gazed around at the amusement park.

"Wow!" said Frankie. "I can't believe my eyes!"

"Well, guys," said Spike, grinning, "it looks like it's. . .

PARTY TIME!"

With Spike leading the way, the monsters headed over to the Swing-O-Rama. When they got there, they were happy to find plenty of empty seats for all of them to ride.

"This is so cool!" shrieked Wolfie.

"Why do you think all those people were in such a hurry to get off?" asked Sadie.

"Beats me," said Spike. "YEE-HAA!"

"Hey!" yelled the attendant. "NO STANDING!"

After stumbling off the Swing-O-Rama, the monsters were on the go again.

"I want to do the Squirt Game!" said Boris.

"Video games!" screamed Sadie.

"Bungee jumping!" roared Fang.

"Bumpy cars!" yelled Frankie.

"Roller coaster!" howled Wolfie.

"To the dunking booth!" cried Spike.

"How does this work?" asked Wolfie when they got to the dunking booth.

Sadie checked it out. "I don't know what the baseballs are for, but if you push this thing here"—and she did—"this clown falls in the ice-cold water."

"Now c-c-cut that out. NO CH-CH-CH-CHEATING," sputtered the very wet clown.

"Hit it again," said Boris, laughing. "That was great!"

DUNK'EM

HIT THE SPOT
SOAK THE CLOWN

At the bumper cars, Frankie's behavior was . . . well, shocking. "Hey," yelled the man who ran the ride. "NO GETTING ZAPPED!"

But no one could
stop these monsters.

Next they went bungee jumping.

After that they broke the moon bounce.

Then they picked up
some souvenirs.

And they never
had to wait in line!

At the water pistol race, the monsters decided they didn't need the targets.

On the boardwalk, Frankie tried to have his palm read.

ZARINA KNOWS ALL
FORTUNES

THE FUTURE REVEALED
FOR AMUSEMENT ONLY

At the slot car races, Fang got a little carried away.

The monsters were having an awfully good time being just awful.

Suddenly Frankie stopped in his tracks. "Hey," he said, "I'm hungry."

"Me too!" howled Wolfie.

"Look!" cried Boris. "PIZZA!!!"

Everyone ran for the food counters. They grabbed sodas and cotton candy, french fries and hamburgers, caramel apples and pretzels, ice cream cones and pizza.

"Okay, kids," said the woman at the cash register. "Who's got the money for all this food?"

The monsters stopped eating. "I think Dr. Fear has money," said Sadie politely.

"Oh," replied the woman nicely, "then I should charge this to Dr. Fear?"

The monsters all grinned and nodded happily.

With their bellies full, they raced off for the rides again.

The fun house gang rode the roller coaster until they were dizzy. They all had a great time—all except Vulture, that is.

"I knew it was a mistake to do this so soon after eating," he groaned.

As they got off the roller coaster, an angry security guard was waiting for them.

"Okay, punks," he said. "The party's over."

But the T-rex had another thought. . . .

"No! Fang! Bad dinosaur!" the whole gang yelled. "Spit him out!"

With a soggy "woof," Fang reluctantly coughed up the guard.

"THAT'S IT!" shrieked the guard, dripping with dino-slobber . . .

"Thrown out of the park!" said Boris.

"Dr. Fear won't be back for two weeks. What do we do till then?" cried Wolfie.

"Where can we go?" said Frankie, sniffling. "The fun house is our home."

"And where will we sleep? Our beds are in the fun house!" said Sadie.

"My blanket's in the fun house!" wailed Spike.

It was all too much for Fang, who began blubbering uncontrollably.

Just then, the headlights of a car shone out of the darkness, as someone pulled into the parking lot.

"It's Dr. Fear!" shouted Spike. "You didn't go away after all! YOU CAME BACK!!!"

"I forgot my passport," said Dr. Fear. "I'll have to catch another flight tomorrow morning. Now will somebody explain to me why you're all out here?"

The monsters blurted out their story to Dr. Fear.

"We're sorry, Doc," said Spike. "It was like we sort of snapped!"

"It isn't easy being cooped up, scaring people all the time," Frankie added.

"Lots of pressure," said Boris, nodding in agreement.

Dr. Fear looked at the gang thoughtfully.

"You monsters caused an awful lot of trouble," he said. "But I guess it's really my fault. I didn't realize you needed a break as much as I did."

Then Dr. Fear broke into a smile. "I've got an idea. How about you all come with me? You know, like a big family vacation."

"Yahoo!!!" The whole gang cheered with joy.

"Now," said Dr. Fear, "I'll have to disguise everyone so we can sneak back into the park." He opened his suitcase and started handing out his vacation clothes.

"The tourists are looking weirder every day!" the ticket-taker said to himself as Dr. Fear and his peculiar guests marched past the gate.

The next morning, a full plane headed for sunny Pago Pago . . .

. . . well, almost full.